POISON DART FROGS

Jennifer Owings Dewey

BOYDS MILLS PRESS

Acknowledgments

My appreciation and thanks go to Karen Klockner, Wendy Saul, Twig George, Mary Sundstrom, and to Jack Cover at the National Aquarium in Baltimore, Maryland.

Left: Lehmann's poison dart frog, *Dendrobates Lehmanni*
Title page: Strawberry poison dart frog, *Dendrobates pumilio*
Front cover (l to r): Strawberry poison dart frog, *Dendrobates pumilio;*
Harlequin poison dart frog, *Dendrobates histrionicus*
Back cover: Strawberry poison dart frog, *Dendrobates pumilio*

Copyright © 1998 by Jennifer Owings Dewey
All rights reserved

Published by Caroline House
Boyds Mills Press, Inc.
A Highlights Company
815 Church Street
Honesdale, Pennsylvania 18431
Printed in Hong Kong

Publisher Cataloging–in–Publication Data
Dewey, Jennifer Owings
Poison dart frogs / by Jennifer Owings Dewey — 1st.ed.
[32]p.: col. ill.; cm.
Summary: A variety of colorful and tiny poison dart frogs living
in the rain forests of Central and South America are pictures in
their natural habitat. Topics covered include: mating habits, natural predators, methods to extract the
frog's poison, and its unique nurturing habits.
ISBN 1-56397-655-2
1. Frogs—Juvenile literature.[1.Frogs.] I. Title.
597.8 /9 21—dc21 1998 AC CIP
Library of Congress Catalog Card Number 97-74194

First edition, 1998
Book design by Amy Drinker, Aster Designs
The illustrations are done in colored pencil.
The text of this book is set in 17-point Minion.
10 9 8 7 6 5 4 3 2 1

For the frogs of the world

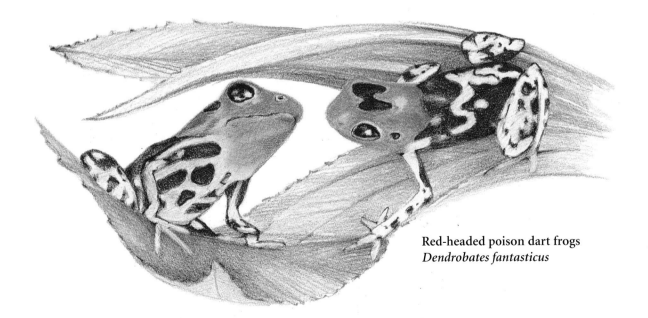

Red-headed poison dart frogs
Dendrobates fantasticus

Phantasmal
poison dart frog
Epipedobates tricolor

Green-and-black
poison dart frog
Dendrobates auratus

Blue poison dart frog
Dendrobates azureus

Poison dart frogs live in the rain forests of Central and South America. Some of these frogs are brown and green, like those often seen in North America. But many are brightly and beautifully colored—in patterns of red, orange, yellow, green, blue, black, and more. They can be spotted or striped or solid in color. And they are very, very small.

Phantasmal poison dart frog
Epipedobates tricolor

Lehmann's poison dart frog
Dendrobates Lehmanni

Silverstone's poison dart frog
Epipedobates Silverstonei

There are over a hundred different kinds of poison dart frogs. One of the tiniest is nicknamed "Buzzer." It is the size of a cricket and makes a sound just like one. Another is called the strawberry poison dart frog because of its bright red skin. It is only three quarters of an inch long. The harlequin poison dart frog is bigger—about one-and-a-half inches long.

It is sometimes chocolate brown in color with an orange "bull's eye" on its back.

The skin of a poison dart frog is slippery and moist. When one of these frogs gets scared or excited, poisons are released through its skin. The poisons of the brightly colored frogs of the rain forest are strong enough to harm or kill other creatures.

"Buzzer"
Demonic poison dart frog
Minyobates steyermarki

Strawberry poison dart frog
Dendrobates pumilio

Harlequin poison dart frog
Dendrobates histrionicus

1   2   3   4   5   6

scale in inches

Strawberry poison dart frog
Dendrobates pumilio

Strawberry
poison dart frog
(bronze variant)
*Dendrobates
pumilio*

Golfodulcean poison dart frog
Phyllobates vittatus

Poison dart frogs can hop, crawl, and climb about freely in the daytime. Most animals learn not to eat them, which helps protect the tiny, bite-sized creatures. If a bird or snake or spider does eat a poison dart frog, it may get sick and die. If it survives, it will remember the bitter taste and numbness in its mouth from touching the little creature and will avoid eating one the next time around.

One of the deadliest poison dart frogs is called the terrible, or golden, poison dart frog. It is found only in a small region of Colombia, South America, and is bright yellow in color. It is one of the three kinds of poison dart frogs used by hunters to make poison darts. The poison has a paralyzing effect, like that of other poison dart frogs, but even more powerful; it is deadly to the touch for human beings. If a jungle snake swallows one of these frogs, the snake's muscles and heart will stop working in minutes, and it will die.

Terrible, or Golden,
poison dart frog
Phyllobates terribilis

Long ago, hunters in some regions of the rain forest learned how to extract poison from these frogs and to recognize which ones had the deadliest poisons. The hunters used the poison on the tips of their blowpipe darts and could kill a monkey or a jaguar in a matter of minutes with just one dart.

Today hunters also use guns. But hunters who use guns may scare animals away with the loud blast. A dart shot from a blowpipe makes no sound. So some hunters still carry blow-pipes, and if they run out of ammunition or want to kill more than one animal, they rely on their old, silent ways of hunting.

Terrible, or Golden,
poison dart frog
Phyllobates terribilis

To catch the frogs, hunters stand in a patch of jungle and imitate frog calls, which sound like the whistles, chirps, and trills of birds and insects. Frogs will hop close to the hunters when they hear the calls. The hunters cover their hands with leaves to protect their skin. Then they grasp the frogs and tuck them into a hollow cane or basket. The frogs stay alive for several days until the hunters collect their poisons.

Three-striped poison dart frog
Epipedobates trivittatus

The hunters have different ways of gathering poisons from the skin of a frog. Sometimes the frog is held down on the ground with a stick, which frightens the frog and causes its poisons to flow. A hunter will then rub his darts in the poisons. Afterwards the frog is released back to the jungle. The frog's body soon makes new poisons to replace the old.

Another method is for a hunter to drive a long stick through the frog's throat and dangle the frog over a fire. The heat of the fire and the pain of the stick draws the poisons out as a thick yellow froth. The hunter then dips his dart point into the foaming bubbles. These frogs do not survive.

Rain falls nearly every day in the rain forest, creating an environment thick with leaves, vines, trees, and flowers—an ideal home for many kinds of creatures, including poison dart frogs. But when the rain is heavy, it can be a threat to the tiny frogs, who hunt for food such as ants, termites, and other small insects on the ground. The streams of rushing water from the heavy rains may sweep the frogs away and drown them.

Strawberry poison dart frog
Dendrobates pumilio

Yellow-banded poison dart frog
Dendrobates leucomelas

Zimmermann's
poison dart frog
Dendrobates variabilis

Bromeliad

Many beautiful plants grow in the rain forest, including one called a bromeliad. The broad leaves of the bromeliad fold over each other to form natural bowls and cups where rain-water collects. These water-filled cups act like a kind of nursery for baby frogs growing from tadpoles into adult frogs. The tadpoles are brought to the bromeliad pools by one of their parents. The tadpoles swim around in the water for four to six weeks until they have grown into tiny froglets who can hop about on their own.

Like many other kinds of animals, poison dart frogs are territorial. The male frog defends his own little area of the jungle. He makes frog calls throughout the day to let neighboring males know that the spot he's in belongs just to him. He might fight off another male frog by wrestling with him and grabbing him around the middle. Or he might push with his strong back legs to move the other male away.

Terrible, or Golden,
poison dart frogs
Phyllobates terribilis

Three-striped poison dart frogs
Epipedobates trivittatus

Poison dart frogs mate several times throughout the year, especially during the rainy season. The male frog makes a certain call to attract any females that might be nearby. A female of the same species will come close to the male and rub her nose against him. The pair of frogs acts out a ritual dance. The two frogs spin in circles, dip their heads, and arch their necks.

After the mating dance, the male leads the female to a moist, well-protected spot under a fallen leaf or a log. There, the mother frog lays a small number of eggs—about two to twelve. Right away, the father fertilizes them.

Dyeing poison dart frogs
Dendrobates tinctorius

Strawberry poison dart frog
(color variant)
Dendrobates pumilio

The eggs must be kept
wet until they hatch. Sometimes a parent frog will soak its
skin in a puddle of water and sit on the eggs. Or a parent
will squirt urine on the eggs
so they won't dry out.

Strawberry poison dart frog
Dendrobates pumilio

Harlequin poison dart frog
Dendrobates histrionicus

The eggs, which are not poisonous, are in danger of being eaten by snakes, insects, or even other female poison dart frogs. Although spiders do not eat the eggs, they are still a threat to the frog parents. The parents stay close to their eggs, and the bright colors of the frogs help keep predators away.

When the eggs hatch after about a month, one of the parents sits in the middle of the clutch, and the tadpoles climb onto his or her back. The frog then hops to a bromeliad or other water-holding plant or tree hollow, where the tadpoles slip into the water.

Strawberry poison dart frog
Dendrobates pumilio

Some varieties of poison dart tadpoles
will eat one another, so the parent may drop
each one into its own pool. Others drop their
tadpoles in small groups into the bromeliad pools
or puddles or tree holes.

The female strawberry poison dart frog visits her
tadpoles every few days in their bromeliad pools. She lays
one or two unfertilized eggs in each pool for the tadpoles to
eat. Tadpoles who aren't fed this way by their parents
will eat the insect larvae and algae they find swim-
ming and growing in their pools of water.

Strawberry poison dart frog
Dendrobates pumilio

When tadpoles are brought to their little pools, they are not yet poisonous, and their skin colors are dull. Their poisons develop soon after their colors develop, over a period of one to three months as they grow into adult frogs.

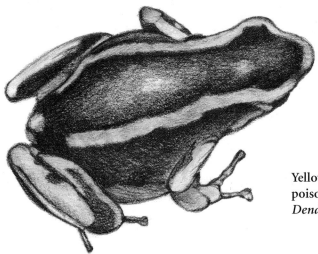

Yellow two-striped Surinam
poison dart frog
Dendrobates trivittatus

Scientists who study poison dart frogs have discovered that if the frogs are born in zoos or aquariums, they never become poisonous. Something special in the rain forest world—probably the kinds of tiny ants and mites the froglets eat—allows them to develop their poisons.

Bassler's poison dart frog
Epipedobates Bassleri

From poison dart frogs to parrots with brightly colored feathers to slithering snakes to panthers with yellow eyes, creatures of all shapes and sizes live in the rain forest. Each of these animals depends on the habitat of a warm, lush, humid jungle for survival. The tiny poison dart frog has a unique place in the rain forest world. It is just one of the countless jungle animals who are so perfectly suited to their environment.

Splendid poison dart frog
Dendrobates speciosus